Network

Christopher Besonen

Published by Besonen Horror, 2021.

To Valentin Bertolino, who illustrated the art that inspired and was used for this book. Also for the fans who just had to know what was happening outside Sphere Court!

Copyright

This is a work of fiction. Names, places, characters, businesses, places, events or incidents are written in a fictitious manner, or an output of the author's imagination. Any resemblance to any actual persons, living or dead, or actual events, is purely coincidental.

All text contained within this book, rather digital or physical, is protected by copyright law. ©2021-2022. All rights reserved unto Christopher Daniel Besonen, the author, courtesy of the Besonen Horror trademark. No unlicensed reproductions of this book may be used, without written consent by Mr. Besonen.

Chapter 1:
Floaters, The First Offering

Nephaniel walked down the hill to the stream at the base of the slope. The three floating bodies made him smirk. One by one, he dragged the corpses across the stream and up the incline across the way.

At the top of the second hill was a series of abandoned mobile homes. Each one was metallic black and attracting sunlight. Nephaniel took the three cadavers and placed them in their places of rest. Once they were secured, he walked back down the hill, crossing the stream, returning to his commune.

The building structure was like that of church, but without windows. The only light in the place emitted from torches that hung from the ceiling. The walls were a fortress of white rocks. Not only did the stones repel the ray from the sun, it also was invisible to the many eyes of the Velocirousel. He had heard their snarls when he was mounting the third corpse. They were predators for the ones who pray. Nephaniel had to be careful when exiting the home of worship.

They were his family and he was their leader to their eternal destination. A place they referred to as, "The Pit." It was Nephaniel who uncovered the whispered about realm. He was a boy who was lost within the woods when he came across the rusty scroll.

Nephaniel was raised beyond the atmosphere of Earth. On a planet later eradicated by The Khartophinites. There, he was taught about a hidden entity on Earth. The rumored being became his obsession, he spent years seeking the one they taught him about. Nephaniel was born with a gift, one that allowed him to speak all languages of Earth, Earth's neighbors and even the dialect of other galaxies. The only one he was ever unable to interpret was the Velocirousel. The carnival carnivores trilled among themselves with lingo of the abyss.

"Rejoice brother, for they went to a better existence. I loved them as my own. They were my own. They were called and they gladly answered. Be merry. Come and talk with me if you must. I'll be in my closet."

The closet Nephaniel was referring to was his prayer room. The space could be spoken into, but any noises that occurred within were silent to the outside. Only he was permitted entry. He often emerged with streaks of black decorating his body. He would slither along the floor while rolling over, speaking in tongues unheard by mankind. The dialogue of the one he sought. His flesh singed, but he was unharmed. He would then writhe himself up to the next chosen family. He would stand himself upright without bending any limbs and would mark them with the mark of ash. Sealing them as the next sacrifice. The creaky door of the closet opening both startled, and aroused, the group that followed Nephaniel's prophecy. Though it was a honor to be picked, death still frightened them. The 'what if' doubts exist with even the deepest devoted at times, but most press on in faith. This was certainly the case with Nephaniel and his people.

The grieved, his name was Tretmor, the only living relative of the recently departed and new ornaments up the hill. He knew better than to approach the closet during prey time. He had tried it once before, which resulted in his death. Nephaniel resurrected him, but he internally wished he had remained deceased. He longed for the end, but there isn't one. All go on in one way or another, he had seen all the others during his time inside the small area Nephaniel had just nefariously invited him to. He knew better than to accept.

The door creaked open, revealing a fluttering eyed Nephaniel. He was muttering. His feet didn't touch the floor, but he was hovering among the others in motion.

"What's wrong with him?"

"Corrina, quiet," Suzette mumbled to the inquisitive child of her's.

"I have seen the light. We must gather more flock. We must offer more sacrifice. He that sleeps, must be woken. Just as we have been awakened!"

Blood dripped from no source onto the foreheads of Suzette and her child.

"You will be his bride," Nephaniel smiled, putting a hand on her shoulder.

He then looked to her child.

"That thing, must be offered."

Suzette nodded to show agreement, holding the hand of her offering.

"He is worthy," she nodded as she closed her eyes, shivering from a chill of enlightenment.

"Go and submit unto him what is his."

Suzette led her child by the hand down to stream and held her under until the bubbles stopped. They had all shared the same dreams and knew the method which they were to use. Bubbles ending equaled completion.

When the child was floating, Suzette returned to feast with her family. They spoke not of what she did, for they considered it a justified deed. A noble cause.

"He without life, wants to live. Once given life, so shall man see his end."

A collective, "amen," arose from those gathered at the supper. Then they all ate and were jolly.

When the sun was coming to be in the morning sky, Nephaniel descended to the open eyed child of Suzette. He took the child to the same trailer as the others, then placed the girl beside all of the rest. He looked at the other trailers and smiled, only two out of four to go to raise the sleeping one. The others were burnt and conjoined together, waiting to be risen. There was still time to go, but every floater meant another spot closer to fulfillment of the buried's rebirth.

Like the closet of prayer, only Nephaniel was given permission to leave the grounds of the compound. His flock were locked inside the structure with only one door to allot egress. The door was operated by a keypad that had no push buttons on the inside, only on the outside. To open the door from within, two attachments had to be on either side of the forehead, the code would then be entered telepathically. Only Nephaniel knew the code to get out. He was told that there was something new and cutting edge, being unveiled at a city nearby.

Nephaniel excused himself from his congregation and went to see what the latest craze was about. He felt like this too was a beginning. Another step forward. He had a different dream than his congregants, one that gave him a parallel mission than just giving the buried one his life. One that involved the ever evolving technology. He didn't understand it yet, but he would. He had to. He was the pivotal being of the end times. Him, and him alone.

"The ethernet. A cord to the future," a woman with a nasally voice explained to Nephaniel.

To watch the two computers communicate was something unheard of but necessary. Nephaniel could hardly contain his excitement watching it occur. When the demonstration was finished, Nephaniel waited for all the other onlookers to fade. When they were specks, he bludgeoned the woman with one of the computer monitors. Taking the ethernet cable, along with her body, he stepped his way back towards the trailers with the burned on dead. The journey was long, but he knew shortcuts. He had to evade detection. His gift of speech also transcended the dimensions. He knew how to split the seams and teleport himself.

"I think you'll do here," he told the smashed in head of the woman, nailing her on top of the caked on victims of his crusade.

"You'll honor him well," he whispered in her bloodied ear, kissing it, while her caved inwards expression stared on.

He walked down to the stream, cleansed the spilt blood off, then went back to his family after hiding the ethernet cable.

"Tell us again about the scroll," Suzette giggled, her eyes cloudy with lust for her groom.

"Gather -"

Suzette stopped him.

"Tell me, in private."

She led Nephaniel to his bedroom. She laid on his bed and listened to him speak, listening to the story she had memorized since she was a little girl.

"I was a lad at the time. Lost in the woods created from the blood of eternal evils. I had ate of their poison, yet I was not sick. I talked with infinite entities who led me to a scroll stuck between two realms, The Gray World and The Pit. It spoke of a coiled being who grows from despair. Grows within the Earth, one who will eat of the Earth on the last day of the planet's existence. They named him, Kommae. The grand pause in time and space."

Suzette groaned, squirming with anticipation. Nephaniel grinned, continuing his tale. He was not turned on by her, but retelling his story always filled him with excitement.

"The term 'comma' derives from the one who is buried's name. He will end the seeping hemorrhage. Creating a void between The Almighty Maker and all that is wicked. Good will cease to exist, supremacy in darkness will be without interference. I shall serve at his right side and you at his left. The dead shall nourish him and be with purpose."

Suzette screamed, her eyes white with ecstasy. Then they turned black and leaked rusty streaks down her cheeks.

"We are the ones who shall tip the scales! We are the blackest spots of the universe! We are the carriers of Armageddon!"

Lightning lit up the hill across the way, helping to fry the piled on martyrs. Suzette levitated. Nephaniel clapped his hands, rejoicing in the thought of the prophecy of the scroll coming to pass. The lightning struck many times, as those cooked on and stacked up sang praises with voices of the undying.

"Doom is glorious!

Glorious is doom!"

Nephaniel sang along the words with them, while Suzette danced around the room. With each flashing crash, their voices unified in volume overpowering the thundering sounds of the approaching storm. The service carried on until the dawn. At the end of the worship, there was an earthquake and Suzette became pregnant with a second child. One that would meet the same fate as her last, when she was again called upon to offer. She named the child Dean. The first son of the eternal seed. Corrina was the first, but she was the first daughter. Nephaniel was surprised to learn of a boy to be bore, but told Suzette that she was blessed to have a male growing this time. A rare and special occasion. She felt honored.

Suzette had first met Nephaniel in 1948. They were colleagues and lovers, many times. She knew it then, just as she still did, Nephaniel was destined to bring mankind to their knees. He had two things that he was relying on, that he now had in his possession. A computer and a way to connect two computers.

When Lucifer fell from Heaven, he created a special lightning. The result was a connection between planet Earth and the lurking dark beings that rivaled Abraham's Lord. Those who lurk provided Nephaniel with the scroll that would shape transhumanism. They had placed Kommae in the ground, half buried in Earth two and three. He was the first Aboriginable, one that was waiting on the Earths becoming the right temperature. He was also waiting on the sacrifices to reach a certain number. The year of his rise would be decades post the year of the ethernet, which was 1973. For now he laid dormant, but the time would come. The thermometer was beginning to sprout among the middle of the court of the nailed deceased.

The first offering had taken nearly a decade of convincing to manifest. Now, they were all okay with drowning themselves one by one. Before the suicides, they collected the people in the images of missing person posters. Like the rest, Nephaniel would drag them up the hill, strategically placing them where he was guided to in his spirit.

He was infatuated with the first one that gave her life for his cause. Her name was Dawna. Nephaniel's sister. The only time he ever shed a tear for someone recently departed was then. Not because of sadness did he cry. He wept with pride at his own ability to manipulate life, the grip of which he would never loosen.

Chapter 2:
A Voice In Lightning

Nephaniel was tinkering with the dials on the CB radio, which were spliced to the computer, which led to a makeshift antenna in the middle of the trailers. It was beside the antenna that the thermometer was starting to grow rapidly, nearly doubling in size in a little over a decade. Different frequencies were achieved, he heard numerous voices, none of which did he care to decipher. He kept running through pitches of sounds until he found the voice that matched one he had heard in a dream. It sounded inhuman, yet was full of knowledge.

"Hello, this is Nephaniel. Earth calling. Do you copy?"

"Loud and clear."

Nephaniel clutched the CB receiver to his heart, praising the name of Kommae below him.

"From which Earth did you state you were calling?"

"Is there multiple?"

The voice laughed, then said nothing. Nephaniel kept trying to reach the voice again, but it refused to reply. He began thrusting his fists at the dried up sidewalls, emptying his frustration on their blackened skin. He was assuming he had blown his important calling. He slept for a month straight, curled up like an infant in a womb. Not visiting the closet, or the portal it opened. His congregation started to assume him no longer among the living.

Nephaniel went on a killing spree once he got out of bed. When he was not crusading, he was trying to reach the voice. He felt that more sacrifices would prove his worth to the whoever the inhuman voice belonged to.

It would be eleven years since the first contact was made. In 1984, the voice responded for a second time.

"This is Nephaniel of Earth. Any copy out there?"

"From which Earth are you from?"

Nephaniel leaped to his feet. He would have swore it imagined, had the voice not kept on.

"Nephaniel, you beam from the second one."

Nephaniel fumbled for correct wording to answer. He sighed, then let it come natural.

"Yes. It is I. Nephaniel of the second. How did you know -"

"What is it you seek, Nephaniel of the second Earth?"

"Wisdom. But also, domination. The darkest of the black souls of mankind. A heart of pure evil."

"You have much to learn, Nephaniel. First, you must modify your computer. I hope you're handy with technology, or things could get bumpy. Like a car thumping over cadavers posing as speedbumps."

Nephaniel listened and applied. Applied and adapted. Adaptation, he felt an attachment to that word. It was what he was doing with Kommae, the sacrifices and eventually humanity. What he was taught, he told his congregation in selective segments. He chose his wordings carefully, ensuring he did not alter their personal quests at all.

By now, the truly heavy with faith were being nailed alive on top of the baked on corpses. Slowly starving, frying, with their heads held high and smiles on their faces. They were extremists, those who were lukewarm continued to drown themselves in the stream as was tradition. The layers were uncountably deep now. Nephaniel had to conform a blacksmith to his cause to make nails long enough to penetrate through the stacked bodies. Three trailers were covered, one still to go.

"Lucifer fell from Heaven, leaving the cosmic streak of lightning which you have tapped to reach me, Nephaniel. The same current runs through your special closet. It travels all through the cosmic oceans, to the intergalactic shores of further realms and future realities. Including, the outer darkness. The fall bridged a gap that was created by The Almighty, allowing the interactions between flesh and spirits, causing a bleeding to occur in realms, creating an eternal expanse of dimensions, each once corrupted in the way Earth one was. What you see in your world, has happened to some degree of a parallel in the first Earth. It is being reversely reflected into the third. Nephaniel, do you know why it is that history acts in repetition?"

The voice posed the question, but denied time for a response.

"Reflections. All events reflect. This is where you come in, I am from the first, you the second. The third shall also be devoured. Now, it is time for the demise of your Earth to unravel. The final corrupting of what Abraham's God intended. Are you willing?"

"I am," Nephaniel accepted with watery eyes.

His eyes full of electric. His major arteries attached to his newly upgraded computer. He raised his hands, as silver overtook the galvanic fluid of his brain. The owner of the voice was now in possession, Nephaniel was but a temporary vessel, but he wasn't aware of that, not yet.

The closet door creaked, then Nephaniel stood before his people, levitating. He outstretched his arms. His eyes flashing like red, silent thunder.

"There is one that is unfaithful among us, my brothers and sisters."

He walked among his crowd, his fingertips dripping silver. A silver mark appeared on Tretmor's forehead. Nephaniel's fingertips seemed magnetized towards the marking.

"Have you lost your faith, brother Tret?"

"Surely not!"

"He says to prove yourself then. Just as your entire family proved their dedication. Come with me and let us talk."

Nephaniel led Tretmor to the other hill, among the outsides of the trailers. This was the only time that any of the members had seen the circle of sacrifice, excluding Suzette and the living nailed in place. They passed the smiling sufferers, ignoring their protruding ribcages poking through epidermis.

"Each of these were given up for what I am to do. For the rising up of he beneath. Will you do what is necessary for the family?"

"I do. I shall."

Nephaniel grinned, then placed a hand on his left shoulder and whispered the mission into his right ear. Tretmor nodded in agreement, two were gathered in unity. A pact of doom.

It was roughly a year later, 1985, when Tretmor was seen again. Not his face, but him doing his life's work. He had gained his pilot's license and was expelling micro metals over the populations. Some call them, "chemical trails." Tretmor covered as much land as he could, then one day when his plane was low on gas he decided to not refuel. He instead crash landed in an ice cream parlor, killing over a dozen.

"What you see in your world, has happened to some degree of a parallel in the first Earth," Nephaniel repeated to himself, when he learned of the deadly kamikaze.

"All things are reflective."

Shortly after Tremor's sacrifice, Suzette left the cult of Nephaniel. She had lost her second child to the waters, ending the abominable birth of the son of Kommae. The loss devastated her leader and she stated she had to leave to mourn. Unable to cope himself, Nephaniel had no choice but to oblige.

Soon after the departure, she met a man slightly older than her. They fell in love and she once more carried a child. She named her Susan, after herself. Being pregnant by a human rather than an entity was an experience she wasn't prepared for, but battled through. Comfortable in trailer courts, the new family moved into one without supernatural connections. Their lot number was 170.

When Susan was not yet a teen, her mother Suzette met another person who would alter her beliefs. Her name was Geneva Shaw, another owner of a trailer park. Shaw shifted her perspectives and it was her that led Suzette astray from what Nephaniel was foreshadowing for good. She had discussed rejoining Nephaniel, but it wasn't to be. She departed one cult, so she could align with another.

The voice was speaking quicker than Nephaniel could write or retain.

"A very wise man was once quoted as saying, 'love is a gift given and received by few, those who received the gift have already been paid.' "

"Nosferatu?"

"Truk Nosmada, prior to his execution."

"Right. The guy from the video from Earth three. Kurt's reflection."

"Correct. Keep up, Nephaniel, these things are imperative. Store them so they are not forgotten."

Nephaniel wrote down the quote, which he recited at Suzette's wedding, claiming all was forgiven.

The day after the honeymoon, Suzette's newlywed was found in chunks. Nephaniel had lured him to the Velocirousel stomping grounds with the help of Geneva Shaw. He was dead well before he heard the first snarl of satisfaction from the beastly attraction. The raptors with the spines of brass that are stuck half in the current realm, half still prehistoric. The ones adjoined by a spinning set of mirrors, that can reflect packs upon packs of snarling, famished birds of prey. Her groom's untimely detaching surely called for a ceremony in which the casket was closed. Suzette would later lie to Susan and tell her that her dad had been cremated. She would also claim no autopsy had been performed, which wasn't a lie as it wasn't needed. Very few could be responsible for such maiming.

The Velocirousel was a beast that became about due to a glitch in time travels. They were crippled by a spell conjured by Geneva, who rid them of their large talons and used them for puncturing her own series of sacrifices. She cast the spell as punishment for disrupting Suzette's happiness. She cared for her partner in depth despite her own efforts in ridding her of her groom. When Suzette met Shaw, her faith tore away from Kommae towards another timeless entity of evil called Htaed, or The Deep. There was a bond of destiny between the two women. Nothing would separate them from their calling. Blood would be shed at the tips of the detached talons. Spilled to empower. Which demigod could disrupt that which was written first? That, was the recently developed game. The Pause versus The Deep. A reflection of the contest of Ian and Ethan.

"My people, when the pause happens, we will be consumed by our buried leader. Those of us who choose to follow, will become as one with darkness. A day is coming when death is no more. When sickness and disease are but a bitter memory. It is coming and I for one want to be a part of it all! To be ahead of the curve. Those who sacrifice will be there with me, and those who we choose to come along with us. You all will be there with me!"

Nephaniel's voice cracked at the end, as did his psyche. He drooled a little, completely engulfed in what he knew he could accomplish. Would accomplish. When he was done giving his doctrine, he went to meditate up the hill. He noticed the trailers had rotated, a sign that his goal was another step closer. He praised the doom of Earth, as did those baked onto the blackened metal. They lifted up the name of Kommae until dawn, then Nephaniel went back down the hill and gathered another drowned family. He whistled happily as he placed the dead in their spots. Once nailed, they all stared up at the ever growing thermometer and sung their songs of reverence.

The voice worked through Nephaniel, controlling him and his moves, but not yet his mind. He spoke to himself often, downloading knowledge through his own vocal chords.

"Nephaniel, have I ever told you about the end of the first Earth?"

"You haven't, yet. I'm keen to hearing about it."

"There was once a space traveler and his daughter, I knew them well. There was also a tree from which paper was derived that brought drawings to life. Schematics had to be precise, or there would be flaws in the creations. The father had lost the girl's mother due to a flawed calculation in the creating of her ship. The girl ended up making monsters with the paper, her folded beasts ended the world. Not a flood like that which occurred during the time of Noah, but a flood which turned the Earth to water."

"You mean the Noah one wasn't caused by water?"

"Not like the first. A cosmic water was used during Noah's flood at the time of your Earth, the second. An unleashing of the full potential of The Deep. This isn't the time to explain this, but maybe another time. Another chapter in a different book perhaps."

"So after the first flood, then what?"

"Then the old was wiped away and the one from who the Earth was taken from returned to carry out the original design. But when seraphim made angels rebel, the old Earth was reborn into the new Earth. Followers of the bible, they call it sin. That which goes against the light."

"Why are you telling me this?"

"I thought that would be the obvious part, we are erasing the light from that which was created by god. Banishing the origin intent."

"I just don't see how an electronic box can cause such a thing. I understand our purpose. I do not understand the how."

"You will Nephaniel of the second. Do not get ahead of yourself. Day by day, we draw nigh.

Chapter 3:
Decoding Earth Three

The voice created a split in a section of Nephaniel's brain. It occurred where the mind connects to the spirit. The entirety of Nephaniel's system was being integrated. Two were becoming one.

"The equator is not what is taught. Yes, it is there in the middle. It separates the second and third Earth. A barrier. Some will say the Earth is flat, some say round, both are true to an extent. Half of the sphere is the second, half is the third. So while they can be considered flat with a firmament, they're also a globe. A mock setup of the intended design. Most modern experts report on reflections of the first Earth, which was entirely circular, though in their arrogance they aren't aware of their flawed views.

The more we progress, the more all the veils of the dimensions will thin. Today, we are going to see what it is like for a separator to cease to be. Nephaniel, are you ready?"

Nephaniel assured himself that he was, then they coded a virtual blade which made a laser splice the retina of his brain cells. Doing so, allowed Nephaniel to peek at the third Earth, taking his soul from his body. Unlike the closet, only his vision was transported this time. Like the voice had told him, the people had been devoured. A woman the size of half of a planet sat baking in the sunlight. Her skin was blackening, sizzling like the ones attached to the trailers around where his physical body was. She was covered in the webs of a daddy longleg, poisoned.

He moved his right arm, time sped up. He moved his left and it rewound. He wanted to see how this Earth came to be and how it would conclude. He had to know. After all, the voice told him that the end of them all coincided with technology and consumption to some degree. He was only able to rewind to where a reality game show was all the rage. One where they shamed obese people and mutilated them to either get skinny or die trying. The show was short lived, the final contestant was who was before him. She had grown and grown, eating all the living beings of the third. She had also eaten of an arachnid that was from somewhere else.

"They're all writing inside of her massive stomach, heating up for the final devour. Carving their obituaries on her insides."

"You mean those she ate stay conscious?"

Nephaniel nodded to himself up and down, then said, "as will you and yours."

When Nathaniel made the connection of what he was telling himself, the program sealed his mind retinas and he was returned to the trailer park. Back to his shell of animated clay.

"What was that which I was witness?"

"An alternate timeline in which Earth three coincides with *The Event*. Altered, but still reflective of our own."

Nephaniel was reminded of Nosmada and the tape he saw from the future. He wasn't sure if he recalled the memory from his own banks, or if he unlocked a file from the core of the voice.

"How many Earths will there be?"

Nephaniel asked himself, but he now realized that when he answered, his voice was that of the inhuman voice. He hadn't noticed before because his mind was closed. This was no longer the case, he was fully open.

"Only four. When our will be done, the next one will be created only for those of the light. We shall reign in darkness forever, together. The holy will be somewhere else. Anywhere else."

"Amen."

"They call the merging of the dimensions the grand hemorrhage."

"What is a hemmoraging?"

"Where did you learn of that term?"

"Another transmission that I intercepted during my seeking of you."

"Irrelevant to the children of the black is what that is. A theoretical shedding of the flesh to equal the faith and power taught by the man on the cross. A battle of interdimensions, all veils will be torn at such a time. The last chance for darkness to overcome light. Could only happen if we were to fail. We won't. It is all hypothetical nonsense. It would mean one got into Heaven without meeting death prior. A hemmor age could stall our consumption, if it was plausible."

Nephaniel spat twice, once for himself, once for the voice in his head. They hated scripture and everything of light. They loathed those who were children of good. Despisers of all things Godly.

"Can anything stand between us and our assignment?"

"Simply wedge. Our fulfillment is impending."

When Suzette was forming a sisterhood with Geneva, Nephaniel was preparing a place for the voice, and The Pause, to be transferred to his reality. He thought he had found a place, but the contract fell flat at the last minute. Things weren't falling in place, so Nephaniel beefed up the unwilling sacrifices once again.

The year was 1985, two monumental things took place that year. The development of something that would commonly be the platform of home computers. As soon as the cult of Nephaniel's heard the name, they knew it was a main component in their race to the finish. Also, the first ever web address was established. Something that would explode and revolutionize the world of tech.

Two years ago, there was another key component announced that would pivot the scheme of Nephaniel and the one within, the GPS system. Human tracking. It is always about control is it not? Has been long before the fall of angels.

Nephaniel had always grown the crop for his people. He also supplied it to the residents of Sphere Court. Like the chemical trails, the food was all infused with metals. All roads lead to the ultimate goal. The rise of Kommae and the continuance of control. He had years left to go before it would be a thought, but every detail of his life was planned. Every path routed to The Network.

Nephaniel stood in the closet, just as he had always done since finding the scroll. The space that was shaped like a coffin. Full of dirt, he would suffocate mirroring being buried alive. During the asphyxiation, meal-worms with fangs on both ends would bite upon him to allow blood to flow to create mud. The watery soil then would seep in the wounds caused by the toothy larvae. When he was dead, he would be brought back and would egress the tomb. While in the spirit world, he could learn about all things. See all the crossovers. Everything truly did happen for a reason . The intersections and reflections were revolving doors of mayhem and bloodshed. The human spirit was highly sought after by the other entities, which meant Nephaniel was a trophy kill. He was hunted by all types of foul creatures.

Aside from providing Sphere Court with nefarious food supplies, he also worked with Geneva Shaw to conjure up metals in all the world's food sources and within the products daily used. Harmful metals were in everything consumed, inhaled and applied. The soils were already sour with the blood of the eternal twins of the first Earth, making organic tainted too. This saturated ground, and what sprouted from it, would play a key role down the road for Nephaniel. Shaw worked with her enemy because she felt whom she served was the grandest of them all. This was not a race for her, it was for amusement.

"So the third world has ended according to the alternate vision, how far from their timeline are we in this Earth?"

Nephaniel interrogated himself, while his congregants were buried in their own piles of dirt.

Six feet, and dying one out of thousands of temporary deaths. This was traditional worship in their temple. This was their devotion. Some went the way of asphyxiate then self drown. Others chose suffocation, embed, then starve. Either way, they all welcomed suffering when alive and after death. Showing happy teeth, they were delivered unto various levels of torment for all their existences.

"Everything in reverse. What you have seen is but a reflection of their end. They end, when we end. They reflect us, we reflect them. All things will serve the purpose of sustenance. What you witnessed was a reflection of what is to come for us all. The Pit awaits."

"Amen."

Two years after Tretmor's offering, a mother gave birth before a mirror. Moxley Snygul was the name scribbled on the certificate. After naming the infant, the mom staggered back to the delivery room. She walked calmly to the window, then threw herself through the glass and fell several stories. Her spinal cord was found penetrating up through the top of her cranium. Her leg bones were shattered to the point of pebble in size.

"Nephaniel?"

"Yes, Nephaniel?"

"Go to the closet."

Nephaniel led himself to the coffin of prayer. The door creaked as it was opened, he went inside. The door closed behind him.

He found himself immersed in a black liquid, unable to see but still with eyes. Possibly reversed ones since everything was dark. There were others sloshing around beside him. They were trying to keep from drowning, as was he. Amidst their struggle to stay afloat, they were all laughing. Singing tunes of conquest. They had made it to The Pit!

When he exited the dirt chamber, Nephaniel fell to his knees and was thankful. Only one word was on his thought waves. He spoke it aloud in both voices.

"Reflective."

Drayton Makkey was out skipping stones when he was last seen. He was observed by a few passerbys around 5:00 pm.

By 6:00 pm, his bloodstream was flowing with a concoction of metals. Nephaniel laid the syringe down, then outstretched his palm. Like the view into the alternate third Earth, his fingers controlled the motions. The voice was doing the same to Nephaniel, unbeknownst to him. He still felt like they were sharing.

"You are a robot," he told Drayton.

Drayton responded as Nephaniel commanded, not verbally but via thoughts and motion.

"You are a robot," Nephaniel instructed, not in his voice but the other.

The inhuman voice's frequency was not that of a human, therefore the brain responded differently to the words. Considering. Computing.

After a grueling session of crab crawls, Drayton began to stiffen. He began to move in robotic fashion, even powering down by the suggestion of a make believe button being pushed.

Dose after dose was given, until Drayton no longer came down from the high of being machine. His humanity had malfunctioned. He was evolving. A precursor to prophecy. Prototype one. He was robot.

Chapter 4:
Branching The Hive

1990. Technology was expanding. So was Drayton and his program-ming. As was tradition, sermons of doom were given to the people of Nephaniel. Only the one speaking was not their leader, it was his new slave, Drayton. His mundane teachings were much longer, which meant they stayed dead and buried longer as they listened. He taught nothing fresh, just memorized sessions.

"The Born Year," is what the inhuman voice referred to the year of 1990.

He was referencing the birth of three key infamous things. The world wide web and The Totter Teether of Sphere Court. Nephaniel no longer talked with his birth given voice. He was overtaken completely, just as much a droid as Drayton.

In '91, Drayton began a contest with the veiled cadaver who drove the black van of Geneva's. The goal was simple, who could kidnap the most sacrifices. The competition was abruptly stopped when Drayton was found slung about in varying directions. He may have thought himself bionic, but the grisly remains that were left behind were still very much human.

Drayton was dragging a woman he had hit over the head, when the start of the carnival song played and surrounded him from all sides. The tune never played in full, adding to the unsettlingly feeling when being stalked by the spinning raptors. Sometimes the music came first, other times it was the menacing snarls. The attacks were swift but merciless. The woman was also found strewn to bits. Part of her skull being located was what led to the half mile of gore being uncovered. Pieces unfound were either eaten or debris in some prehistoric dimension. It was Plonti Jeppaheimer and his hound who stumbled on the scene of scraps. He had let his mutt gnaw an entire leg bone before reporting the discovery to authorities.

Nephaniel's new computer was only advanced beyond the current rate of technological advances by a month, maybe two, max. The one behind the voice had the know how, but necessary inventions lagging were crafting a detour.

In the early to mid 90's, home internet surged in popularity. A monumental moment in the computer realm. Home computers connected in invigorating ways. Nephaniel's operating system ran on a supernatural current, allowing him to make vital connections. He could now reach the further regions such as the outer darkness. Instant messaging allowed widespread recruitment.

Dozens of flights took to the air to distribute metallic toxins expelled from kamikaze planes. This was just as much a tradition as the constant demises during the sermons. New members meant the older ones moved closer towards adopting extremism. The door was consistently revolving.

The internet opened up the gate to potential followers, but also constructed an entryway for the one behind Nephaniel to plan for his physical arrival. It was no longer enough to be in control, the voice needed to be!

Moxley boarded the bus to head to her scheduled field trip. Her destination was a maze of animatronics. It was sometime in late Fall, so the theme was spooky. She started with a group, but ended up completely isolated. Just her and the robots.

The maze was dark, lights pulsated from the ceiling in sync with the Industrial and Dance remixes that blared from unseen speakers. The versions of the songs were part pulsating, part slow and forbidding.

Moxley rubbed the sweat from her palms on to her pants as she walked. Every corner had a jump scare. Some sprayed her with water, others reached out to claw her direction while blowing air horns.

After miles of dead ends and leaping machines, she found herself in a winding hall of mirrors. There were no mechanics here, but every one of the reflections showed her in a different outfit. Each were distorted in some way. Everything she did, the other hers in the mirrors did opposite. Then without warning, the mirrors shattered and animatronic versions of her, down to her exact outfit, began to give chase! Their jaws grew wider and wider, until there was nothing but vast mouths at her heels. Any screams that she let out were overpowered by the loud music.

By time she found her way out of the maze, the bus was boarding to leave. Nobody else had experienced what she had. She had entered a parallel reality during her visit. She didn't tell anyone what had happened that day, but she never did rid herself of the scars left by the teeth of the computerized Moxleys.

The year was 1999. Wireless fidelity was the burning topic. The net had opened up all sorts of avenues. Like all things, there were those who chose to corrupt its nature and use it for unorthodox purposes. With light, there's always a shadow. The internet was no exception to the rule.

Nephaniel worshiped in the closet entombment daily. His glimpses of The Pit less and less, eventually fading altogether. Things went on as usual. Families joined the cause, families were drowned and families were nailed as living offerings to the trailers. Some had requested to be skinned alive, then placed and left to emaciate. Prolonging equaled allegiance, the concept remained unchanged. All sacrifices were given with smiles.

One congregant was programmed in a similar fashion to Drayton. The major change was Nephaniel used the brain splicing laser to manipulate the memory cells of the vessel. The progression process was much shorter this go around. Tasks started small, but vastly got intricate. By the finale of '99, the fresh bot and the veiled driver were competing for numbers. A legion were slain. Klyne County flowed red with ritualistic oblation.

Moxley washed her hands then went to wait for her adopted mom on the school sidewalk. Hours passed, still her ride never showed. The staff had all went home, leaving her abandoned.

It was nearing dusk when she begin to walk home, alone. Her legs were sore from bite marks, but she forced herself to be tough. Her calves flowed with blood which made her socks squishy. She got lost along the way and ended up at a gas station ran by a cranky guy in a wheelchair.

"Pardon, but may I use your telephone?"

"Did you give glance at my disability, girl?"

"I would never," Moxley spat in offense.

"Make it quick," the man demanded as he slammed the phone down.

Moxley dialed her house, but was extremely unsettled by the other end being answered with a voice that was identical to her own.

"Hello? Snygul home answering."

"Who is this?"

The person on the other end of the line giggled, "I think you know who I am."

Moxley heard her adopted mom's voice in the background asking who was on the phone. The receiver clicked, then dial tone was heard.

Moxley hurried home, hitching with someone without considering the dangers. Thankfully, the one who gave her a lift wasn't a creep and genuinely was trying to assist a kid in need. The ride took twice as long as she expected since the driver avoided the most southern route. He did so out of superstition stemming from whispered warnings about that stretch of blacktop.

Moxley questioned her mom once she got home, but was given the run around. Her mom was confused by the accusation and couldn't fathom there being a second Moxley. Whatever that call was about, she and the other her were the only ones aware of it. Could there be a duplicate? Does everyone have another them? Moxley stayed up that whole night pondering questions of uncertainty.

Kipley wondered onto the grounds of the Nephaniel compound. He wasn't sure where he was as he had ingested an alkaloid from the trees surrounding Sphere Court. He had walked for hours to get where he was, though time was lost upon him while he was tripping. He thought he had hallucinated a monster in the poisonous forest there, one connected to a pogo stick.

He was coming down and feeling nauseous. Suddenly, he heard the skipping tune of a circus theme and felt the sensation of being stalked. Like the apparition before, he assumed it imagined by the substance.

The moonlight shone through the looming twigs overhead, making everything enshrouded. He heard snarling, but from where couldn't be pinpointed. It sounded surrounding. In an instant, he saw two translucent dinosaurs watching him. Their snake like eyes peered at him, hungry and calculating. Unaware that he was seeing reflections cast from the mirrors of the midsection of the Velocirousel. The true assaults came from the sides. Kipley was in half, and getting torn further, before he had time to process that he was prey. Like the pogo stick monster, neither of the things he saw were a result of hallucinating.

Chapter 5:
Tinier Mechanics And The Normalizing Of The Downlookers

Many sat on the eve of 2000 and awaited a blanket of outage. Rumors had been uttered about a grand scale plunge in darkness. While everyone was chirping on phones that shared the same shades as a bumblebee, Nephaniel was dancing around the circle of trailer in the nude and on fire. He vocalized lovely melodies as he maliciously melted.

"Doom is glorious!

Glorious is doom!"

His phrases were echoed by those pinned to the sides of the mobile homes. His flesh seared to ash. Lasers shot from the eyes of the deceased outer wall ornaments, giving way for the form behind the voice to bring his presence to Earth two. His name was Zyxira. The original artificial intelligence. The beams printed him into the physical. When he was complete, the flames extinguished themselves and the sacrificial printers died another time.

Zyxira was mainly blue with silver lining, but orange flashes could be seen periodically.

"Looked like a nightmarish rave," the android dryly pointed out to himself.

He rolled around in the clay of the Earth to cover his exposed internals. Once covered, he molded himself after the image of Christ, but maintained the vocal progressions of Nephaniel. The created had become creator, soon to turn destroyer. The trailers shifted, another step in the unlocking. The thermometer was now caressing the atmosphere. It turned from gray to yellow.

Computers, televisions and just about any other imaginable electronic was becoming thinner and more compact. The age of tech was rapidly progressing. People were getting accustomed to looking down. This wasn't anything new, readers had been doing so for centuries. The exception was the microwaving of the steel cells that were being pumped into humans per the air, food, drink and applied products. Waves transmitted by the handheld devices were helping to heat up the micro coils swimming the DNA pathways. Very sluggishly, metal was duplicating metal and replacing skin! The transformation was under the dermis, for now.

Zyxira molded together the severed head of Nephaniel and brought it before his people. They rejoiced at his giving of his life. Their new leader fed them a long proverb of a tale about how the former valiantly gave up his living condition. Each member was then commanded to look Nephaniel in his lifeless eyes and gouge their own sockets in honor. Kipley's parents noticed their son missing once the gougings begin. They were the newest members and had been buried for days.

"He should be here to partake."

"When was the last time you seen him?"

"If I may interrupt, he is running a task for me.

Also, it is your go," the dark messiah butted in.

They took their turn without question. They would never see their son again, even if it were opportunistic. Zyxira collected their offerings in a tithing bucket he had acquired. A name was soldered in it: 'Hellstone.'

Zyxira then brought the trailer decorations to life using the wet electricity, removed their minds then killed them back off. He wired the plates of eyeballs to the brain cells and hooked them all up to the computer he helped Nephaniel build back when he was just a voice. He recoded their structures again and again until he had the correct sequence. When he was done, the computer came alive. Connections were made back into the baking dead. The computer spoke through the mouths of the cadavers as a choir of vocalizations. They all collaborated with the same tone. The timbre of Lucifer.

Three hundred and sixty five days to the day of the mysterious call, Moxley went to an airshow. She liked to watch the jet engines roar, she would smile large and cover her eardrums when they did their flybys. At some point, she was separated from her adopted mom. After thirty minutes of frantic looking, she found her by the small airstrip where they were giving flying rides to the children. She walked up to her adopted guardian and put her head on her shoulder.

"I'm tired. Been looking everywhere for you."

"Get away from me," the woman squirmed, shoving Moxley away.

"Mom?!"

"How? You -"

Her adopted mom put her hands over her eyes and rubbed hard enough to cause Keratoconus. After an intense rub that left her seeing blotches, she finished her sentence.

"You just went up in that plane," she pointed at the biplane doing tricks in the sky.

"That wasn't me. I'm right here!"

When the plane landed, only the pilot exited. He looked at Moxley was disbelief.

"How incarnation?"

Moxley screeched at the clouds above and stormed off. She felt insane. There was certainly a second her and nobody had a smidge of explanation. The only one convinced was her, but questions were definitely forming after the airshow occurrence.

She walked until her legs began to feel numb and rubbery. She thought she was near the gas station from before, but the scenery didn't look the same. The more she looked around, the less familiar things became. A twig snapped from somewhere behind her. Then, she heard a snarling. Eyes were on her, many of them. Her ears filled with the intro of a carnival, then she saw her reflection in the mirrors behind the spinning raptors. Electricity shot from the eyes of her other, which switched their places.

Moxley recognized where she was almost instantly. The maze was very distinct in appearance. The music was the same as before, but it was more composed of varying mechanisms in presentation. Arrows illuminated the pathway through the halls, making it less of a maze and more of a guided trail. Moxley was led to a gymnasium. Once she stepped inside, the walls sealed over.

Strobes lit the vast room in flashes. Within the abrupt lighting she could make out a giant face across the ceiling. She was feeling ill once she realized that she was staring in to her own face. Her mouth was open, then her teeth started to wriggle. Each tooth dislodged from the gums and came down and chased Moxley around the gym. The long roots dangled everywhere, but never once did they entangle. As each tooth followed her, they almost looked as if they were dancing to the bizarre music that was playing. A piece of the wall opened up, revealing more arrows that if followed would take her away from the gym. She ran to, then through, the opening.

The strobes continued via the arrows that lined the walls of the new pathway. The teeth slithered behind her, bouncing along the roots that connected to the gums somewhere else. She didn't wonder how far the roots could extend, she didn't have time to think. The teeth were digging through her clothes and sinking in her flesh. With every connection there came a shock. They were acting as tasers! As liquid electric flowed through her mind's eye, she was able to see through the eyes of the other her. To her dismay, she watched as her step mom was beckoned to the woods around Nephaniel's commune and then ripped to shreds by the Velocirousel. As organs were burst as they were chewed through, Moxley began to seize up. Electricity still being pumped, she blacked out and entered a coma.

Chapter 6:
Virtual Grooming

For decades the military had used virtual reality for mock practices. In the early to mid 90's, the tech was introduced to the arcade industry. Players were astonished by the ability to be in one realm, while actively existing in another. Kids and adults both overfed quarters into gaming components to escape to the places offered.

In 2010, the virtual reality was expanded widely via the video game industry. Users could now sit on their couch while being fully emerged in another life, place and series of events. Each game released was a hit among gamers.

The spirit of Nephaniel looked out in a similar manner as the VR, take away the fact he was not in control. Zyxira had replaced his epidermis layer, but the core of Nephaniel remained. Watching as the prophecy was being fulfilled beyond his grasp of control. For a power hungry fascist, this was Hell.

The blind congregation listened to the sermons of the hidden blue android. They passed a plastic bag to one another, along with the fresh on the market VacGlove 1000. They passed themselves out, one by one. When they awoke, it was on to the next. If they didn't wake after six minutes, they were checked for pulse. If no pulse, it was on to the next anyways. All who had ever been a cultist alongside Nephaniel were loyal unto demise. All, but Suzette Bailey. She was a traitor to the faith. Zyxira would make her pay, which would add to the damage of Nephaniel's narcissistic soul. He desired revenge to be at his mercy. He couldn't think badly of Zyxira, they were the same entity now.

'Greater is he who is in thee when it comes to ruling the world,' Zyxira assured him within his own thoughts.

A popular electronics company had made a free network where people could go and hang out virtually. It wasn't the greatest thing, but it was the alpha of groundwork for what Zyxira had up his motorized sleeve.

Social media had paved the way for face to face interactions to appear obsolete. Reducing the importance of family and friend fellowship. Credit, debit, cryptocurrency, it all led humanity by a leash down the path of what was foretold in the scroll Nephaniel was destined to find. A world without the need for profession, status or God. A realm made in man's image. More and more were marching the streets demanding equal treatment. In a make believe reality, ran off the imagination of the masses, anything would be achievable. Equality, world peace, even immortality.

While political attendees from all countries attended an annual summit, the masqueraded droid threw the doors open to their meeting spot. He walked in like he would soon own the place, and he would, in the near timeline.

"Who is this?"

"How'd you get by security?"

"What is this intrusion?"

Zyxira held up his fluttering hands to shush the inquiries. Those in attendance were taken back by the boldness of the stranger.

"Gentlemen of the third, I am that which is most high. The mountains shiver at my voice. I am that I am."

"You stroll in here and expect us to accept that you're God?"

"Not god. An improvement of such a being. Bringer of peace and equality. Gather. You have all heard my message in one way or another. I am he that blossoms fruition. Sit before one that cannot perish. I, and I alone, am a planet shaker. Even heaven bows before me. I shall hold the reins of the planet in my palm."

Whispers arose among the men seated before the olive skinned man with a beard.

"Your arrogance isn't welcome here!"

"The nations will bow before me willingly, or through brute force. Look in my eyes and know that I am thy solution."

The other men then shared a collective mesmerizing experience. The metals in their brains were responding to the frequencies spoken and under manipulation of the disguised bot.

"We have matters to discuss. Surely you can allow time for discussions? We can promise to consider."

"Three days from today, I will return to each of you. Each of you will stand before me and submit alliance, or face annihilation."

Zyxira left a disc behind. On it, there was a presentation he had recorded for them. He referenced the idea behind social media shifting towards a virtual universe that would run along with the waves that the newly revealed 5G network consisted of. His claim was that the waves needed an upgrade from a mineral that he possessed that could reach the cosmos, even entities in other dimensions, if handled properly. By the end of his suggesting, not a single man at the meeting opposed. Within his vocal progressions was further subliminal contrivance.

Three days later, Zyxira visited each of the leaders of Earth two personally. They all signed a treaty with the seductive robot. The treaty tackled all current issues that were the hot topics at the world meeting. What he was proposing solved it all. It ended climate change and emissions, inequality, disobedient citizens and a string of other threats that the current leaders liked to gaslight. It was a genius manifesto. Speaking with the tongue of Nephaniel, Zyxira was able to speak the dialects of each leader he went to see. He knew how to persuade, he talked in algorithms. He was in control now and his first course of action was the slow, silent removal of all religious doctrines. It would happen over time. There were no other gods to be worshiped. He had cometh. He deemed himself worthy to be praised. Idolatry would not be permitted once he unveiled The Network.

Moxley awoke from her coma without any memory of the incidents that had resulted in her deep sleep. She moved forward like all must do and began a job hunt.

Moxley was denied a few rewarding job offers due to her doppelganger. Some resulted in problems with the law. The other her was determined to give Moxley a terrible rep and life. Moxley would show up places unannounced and would have already been there that day. It was as if the other Moxley were always walking just ahead of her. Was she the shadow? Who was who? No answers were uncovered, only more oddly stacked coincidences. Her frustration grew, as did the ruined opportunities and relationships. She confided in her step mom, but their discussions only meant more perplexity for them both.

Chapter 7:
The Network Beta, Odd Bulletin Trio, Introduction To 6G

The worth of the paper dollar was thinning. With finances in ruins and inflation on the rise, another era of depression seemed to be lingering in the near future. Violence was increasing as was intolerance and the cancel culture. Nobody was left alive from the cult of Nephaniel. They had reached the number of bodies needed to be attached to the circle of trailers. The thermometer was orange by this point in time. What was necessary now, was the powering of The Pause. Spirits of mankind ran on a special type of electron, it was time for the best networking Earth had ever seen. Soul unification would awaken the buried one.

All TV programs were interrupted. Their broadcasts now tuned in Zyxira and a pile of corpses. He stepped on them, deeming them worthless since the sacrificial count had been met. These were the murdered unwilling prior to the thermometer turning a darker color.

"People of the third. I am Zyxira. I am eternal. I am less flawed than those idols that preceded me. They were good, but I am beyond them. They talked where I will walk. I will outstretch my palms and change will prevail."

Red lasers began to bounce off the walls of the compound behind him. Their source, were the retinas of the scattered dead. Wherever the transmission was being received, shared the same lasers.

"In your hands, you will find a pair of goggles. We are entering a trial phase of a better tomorrow."

Zyxira put his own set of electro spectacles on, then took his throne among those who had dared to tap in. The beta was a demise trap. Glitches were everywhere, many of them were brought to life as living creatures. Smoke poured out from ears of some of those battered by the glitches. Their mind matter literally frying within their cerebrums. The liability for those who died as a result was zero. They had chosen to put on the headgear. It was an enter at your own risk type of thing. Almost none of the testers survived, which bothered Zyxira not a bit. He made mental notes and worked out how to try again.

The second time that Zyxira appeared on television, he was accompanied by a background of dancing corpses. Like the initial testing, those chosen were not random, a dent in their pinkies from their cell phone usage marked them as the subjects to use. The laser eyes didn't print goggles this time, instead those tuning in were shot with lasers coming out from their screens. The lasers were beamed directly into their sockets. This time, tapping in was mandatory. There was no clause for safety. It was the way of the robot, or be murdered for opposition. Zyxira couldn't be beaten, so he had to be joined. Even glitchier than the previous version, everyone who tapped in was brain fried within minutes. Not even a single survivor made it out of phase two.

Zyxira had infiltrated the planet. Corrupting religions, governments, scientific research. He had been doing so for years while he was afar on another planet. He used pacts made with Lucifer and the glass demons to put his metal finger in all walks of life. He crept in like Death had in ancient Egypt at the time of Moses and the plagues. Those without a blood covenant with The Almighty had no covering of protection then, there was none for those without it now. He had been working through the supernatural electricity long before contact was made between him and Nephaniel. It was his kingdom come. The achievement of prophecies.

Clogged arteries were cleared by nanobots. Miniature versions of Zyxira actually. The tiny robots cured cancer and other terminal illnesses. One nano injection was life changing. Curing wasn't the only change going on, the bots were also altering the DNA of the patients. Making it so those with his blood could be patented as his trademarks. Unable to accept a jab? Fret not, for you could simply eat or drink of the micro bots also. The only excuse for not partaking was disobedience! Failing to obey always ended in fateful "accidents."

It was all the metals put into the bodies that had caused the sicknesses and diseases that the nano robots were cleansing. A continuous web of deceit. Every string was strung by the android. The prophecies were commencing to fire on all cylinders. Nephaniel's spirit was seeing it all unfold at the hands of another.

The third time Zyxira appeared on the TV sets of the chosen, it was done in infomercial fashion. He was walking before those pinned in sacrifice onto trailers. They were alive, but clearly dead.

"Need a quicker connection to the other world?"

"YES," the deceased audience around him robotically responded, their retinas full of lasers.

"Need to raise your personal vibration to match the changing realms around you?"

"YES."

Lasers began to beam from the chosen into the sets of transmission. They were in a trance and mesmerized. Networking with the talking sacrifices.

Zyxira wriggled his fingers and the screen switched to the antenna beside the thermometer. The antenna was glowing red and shooting up past the firmament, surrounding both Earth two and three.

"Long ago, an angel fell. In his falling there became an electric that is wet to the touch. We refer to it as 6G. The final phase of telecommunications. Are you ready?"

"YES," those tuned in at home synced up with the murdered spectators.

Zyxira closed his open palms and the minds of the viewers were transported to an improved version of The Network.

"Welcome to experience 2.0, building a creation of incomprehensible wonders. Thou wilt is not denied here. Think it, be it. Ascend from mere beings of breathing clay. Be beyond your limited intent. Receive me, for I have prepared a place for you. I give unto thee, The Network! Perfection that surpasses the flawed land known as heaven."

Only half of the viewers' minds sizzled, to which Zyxira toasted to the spirit of Nephaniel as a much needed improvement.

"A tightening here, a recode there. Nephaniel, cheers! Our will be done."

Moxley missed her adopted mom's funeral.

"We called you. Spoke with you too. You urged us to go ahead without you, ma'am."

Moxley gritted her teeth. The call log was presented to her, but she didn't need to see the phone number to know they weren't lying. The two minutes and thirty six second backup proof of call length needed not be shown as evidence neither. It was the other one. Her mimic. Clone? Double? Copy? Twin?

She was also informed that autopsy results had already been released to her. She wanted to know the cause of death, but they only had one copy to give out and the other Moxley was already in possession of it. They found her second request suspicious. She knew any details about what had happened would probably get her locked in a loony bin. She left quietly, waiting until she was outside to shriek with grievance.

Chapter 8:

Debugging The Network, Period Of Widespread Expansion

Zyxira stood in front of a shattered mirror. He had busted the reflector due to his irritation of his failing Network. He spent days studying over the schematics to see no flaws. It was improved yes, but was still prematurely killing fifty percent of those who connected.

"Where am I missing the error? What is the answer?"

"Glass," the voice of Geneva informed.

"What?"

Zyxira turned around to see the once busty black woman standing in the doorway. Her arthritic hands were petting against two demons on her back. In the forehead of one was a glass particle, the other had a piece of glass embedded in its right hand. Geneva plucked both pieces of glass and presented them outwards to the concealed droid. The demons vanished.

"Your error is in the infrastructure of the motherboard. You are using metal that is causing too much conduction. You didn't consider the galvanic's sensitivity. Like your special electric and cosmic minerals, I can offer a supernatural material, at a cost, that will resolve your issues."

"Name it."

Geneva walked up to him and whispered in his ear. Zyxira agreed and was supplied with the solution to debug The Network.

Another broadcast was sent out. Zyxira stood in front of the camera with a plastic bag over his face. On his shoulder was a 5 Triple Zero vacuum. He was willingly suffocating at the suck of the eight tentacled invention. Unable to render the vocals of Nephaniel, Zyxira spoke to his crowd telepathically. He was speaking over the waves of the liquid electricity caused by Lucifer's rebellious actions. The wet electric beamed from screen to the fluid within the cerebral systems of the viewers.

'My family, perk your understanding of The Network. I have been working hard towards making my creation safe and effective. Behold, The Network!'

Not only was he talking inside their thoughts, he was also controlling the flock and making them put in laser printed contacts. Ready or not, The Network was waiting!

The virtual existence was vastly improved on this go around. Third time's the charm, only roughly fifty lives were lost. The Network didn't kill them, they took their own lives so that they would never leave the other realm. Zyxira didn't care about tolls, but he cared very much about acceptance. The devotion of a few let him know the world was next. Nephaniel had a new suicide cult, which he wasn't leading. There never was a charlatan like Hiro's robotic masterpiece. Lucifer may deceiveth the whole world, but Zyxira would inherit it. All Nephaniel could do was witness.

The nations were under the droid's rule within the span of thirty days. Everywhere he went, still reflecting the exact features as the Nazarene, Zyxira was widely liked. They opened their homes and families to the new world ruler. He said what the masses wanted to hear and meant to keep his promises. He knew how to allure, much like the boa in Eden's Garden. He pitched accelerating to another reality and his listeners responded by begging for a serene existence, disregarding thought of the costs. If it could be, it should be, was the general attitude. Peace was coming, but like all calms, storms lingered behind.

Zyxira traveled far, recruiting people to join his Network. Some declined, such as the Miscreated Allegiance who were responsible for the Pro Campaigns. He let their rejection slide without repercussion because they still rejected being human. Transhumanism, it was what Nephaniel knew was the term of the future. The sever of God's bloodline. Zyxira knew it too and was more than delighted to destruct.

Chapter 9:
Streaming With The Grain, Switchery The First

The Network took Earth by surprise. All consoles had to buy into the game to even try to think about staying afloat. There was no comparison to what it offered. With the reflective parts of demons at the center of it all, it was existence without limitations. You could do anything, be anything. If you could imagine it or dream it, it was possible. The contacts overtook all senses. Like an undying buzz, those who connected were living out their fantasies in every way and getting euphoric effects from it all. The contacts emitted itty bitty flakes that would grow wings and suction cup mouths. Attaching to the stems of the mind, they were manipulating the galvanized fluid that the brain runs on. They flooded the users with dopamine to keep them subdued. There was no need for reality nor Heaven, The Network was paradise on Earth. Nothing else mattered during that first wave. Living entranced was the way. The poor became rich, weak were strong, shyness transferred to bravery. Thousands quit their jobs, collapsing the already failing economy. This was the ultimate escape. The eternal drug. A big bonus was the fact that no extra gadgets were needing to be worn to tap in, only the eye contacts. Zyxira was far beyond the curve of anything other technological companies could offer. He was editing reality.

Wars raged between all sides. Humans versus hybrids. Race leery of race. Triggering media reports that attempted to ignite outcry were rampant. The murder rate soared all over the third Earth. While bombs were detonating, blades were slicing and guns were blazing, Zyxira overtook those within The Network. He used the rise of the chaotic to usher more and more in. Thousands complied. They stayed in a coma like state somewhere in the throes of imagination, while he had them physically withdrawal nanobot particles from their DNA and infect their relatives, roommates, neighbors, anyone within injection range who weren't sure of unquestionable compliance. Once the metals hit the bloodstream and combined with the metals already stored, the galvanic liquid within their brains acted as a magnet to transport the unwilling to The Network. The coded spell of Zyxira was rapidly engulfing like an eclipse. Night was falling over God's creation. Nephaniel's spirit found it all wondrous despite his self mourning.

One taste of Network and you were converted to the lifestyle. Nobody wanted anything but what was offered in the other realm. Reality was replaceable. At the admission of the soul, one could literally gain worlds. At the disposal of freedom, what was once daydreamed could be tangible in a millisecond. Praying? Reading? Practice? Work? All definitions of fading memories. Ones that would never beg to be conjured. The governments began to supply those linked up with income to pay their bills without ever needing to unplug. They enjoyed their peoples being sedated and in perfect order. What they had always strived to have was proving doable. It was out of the hands of mankind and in the fingers of a robotic charmer. The leaders were nothing more than reflections of Nephaniel's spirit woes. They all had no choice but to love and accept the one they loathed.

He may have looked like a twin of Christ, but Zyxira encouraged anything that was contrary to letters in red bold inside the Bible. Debauchery exalted itself. He who could not sin refused to recognize commandment breaking for what it was. He called God's Word fiction and mocked the text in his podcasts of recruitment.

The Network became an unsafe place. Crimes thought left behind began to spill over. Virtual security detail included a physical one, one that sent armed dilophosaurus to the location tracked by GPS. Physical and mental torture would then be implemented to teach a lesson to the inflicted. Peace was canon in Network, while reality was bathed in the shedding of blood and the spreading of fearmongering. A pack of the crested dinos were lost somewhere in time.

The reflector parts of Geneva's pets had made it possible for two deals to be struck. Due to Zyxira's often bouts of suffocation at the arms of a vacuum, Nephaniel's spirit disengaged from the android who was in full control. He was still trapped inside, but they were now two entities rather than a merged duo. The demons deflected the conversations so that each individual entity could be spoken to without the other's awareness.

"Your sheep help me when the times comes," Geneva had whispered physically.

Spiritually, Geneva had made a hushed deal with the spirit of Nephaniel.

'I'll redirect the circuits of the one controlling you so that places can be switched periodically. He will power down unknowingly every night so that your personal doings cannot be retained. In return, you drop your vendetta against my sister in darkness.'

The spirit agreed, though the agreement was falsified. Suzette had to pay. Her time would come, as would his.

Chapter 10:

Twelve Months In The Life Of Willee Mahkray

Willee Mahkray was a man of serenity. A witty man who had fought the cancerous battle and came out victorious thanks to nano injections. He had one year left before retirement. Thanks to a company with a fruit as their symbol, Mahkray was able to handle technology and its many advances. The gadget that kept him up with the times had also made him a Downlooker.

He was called into HR's office upon his arrival on a Monday morning. He was drinking his caffeine grounds as the manager enlightened.

"Willee, the world is a different place than it used to be. Barely recognizable from the place we once knew, eh? Anyways, The Network is changing things. Microchips and processors are the now, and the tomorrow. Basically, this drawn out speech boils down to one bullet point. We either move with the times or we are obsolete. There is no need for the stop of physical theft, what we have to do now is protect assets within Network. You'll be compensated double too. There's a new way to pay, buy or sell. You hear of it yet?"

"Bless your joyful soul, you must think I was pushed out of my momma just yesterday. Yes, I am well aware of the bonfires of cash and the new implants."

"Get yourself chipped," Chief dictated as he plopped a business card down on the desk between them.

"I'll return soon. Is it a painful procedure?"

"A necessary one."

Willee returned energized. He could feel the electrons multiplying within his bloodstream. He not only felt younger, but looked it too. He was abruptly suspended in metamorphosis.

"That chip contains everything there is to know about you. Medical records, eating habits, whereabouts, it monitors everything. You're a walking GPS."

"Great. Now I can't do anything in privacy without someone spying in on me."

"We're all in the same ship. The entirety of civilization will soon be part of this machine. Changing into something more than human."

"Never in my early days did I think I'd see the erasure of people."

"Well, we are survivors, Willee. We endure what we must to stay afloat. Follow me, I'll show you how the new way works. We can problem solve as we go."

With the implant, there was no requirement of the contacts that most were using. The chipping began to spread like wildfire.

Mahkray patrolled The Network. He had to get used to the cyber aspect, but he was evolving mechanically inside so it came naturally. The implanted microchip was updating his galvanic fluid to acquire the knowledge needed to properly utilize The Network grids. He surveilled the realm to stop hackers from stealing Network identities.

By lunchtime, Willee was already feeling exhausted. He felt hungry, but anything he tried to digest was rejected. The only thing that settled his hunger was downlooking. If he took the slightest glance away from his phone screen, he would feel hollow and suicidal. His body could feel the pull of the other realm. It wanted to worship, it needed to Network!

His direct manager strolled through the door to their shared office, shortly after Willee had his crumpets and caffeinated beverage.

"I have news."

"Bad or good?"

"Better have a seat."

Mahkray was filled in about what the mission was. He would be offered a promotion to be active in The Network working to carry out arrest warrants on a group of digital terrorists who were overtaking sectors of Network and turning them to warzones.

Willee took the promotion and easily worked with his team to take down the subjects from the warrants. Though carried out properly, something seemed strange with it all. He was an unnatural choice for such a task, not to mention it being past his scope of rank. It almost seemed like a deliberate method of distraction. Mahkray wasn't a steel man yet, still he tried to ignore his humanly intuition but it remained.

One day while working to review surveillance system footage, he witnessed himself performing physical work duties while he was supposed to be taking down those making hack attempts. What he would see, confirmed all suspicions. It was all off, every bit of the warrant enactment was simulated. He had to watch several times before it finally sank in. He wasn't in control of his physical self while in The Network. His movements pointed towards robotics. He took the evidence to his manager which resulted in his files being ransacked and all proof deleted. He was then put on a leave of absence pending an immediate medical review.

Willee spent the next week investigating his neighbors. Nobody on his block was leaving for work, or any other events, but they all had vivid memories of their days. Their responses indicated that they thought they had physically went somewhere else, when really they were actually plugged in. Like had happened with him, the worlds were merging. They were subjected to rewiring of the conscious! The Network was responsible for widespread schizophrenia. Network, was actually a transference between spirit and physicality. He would develop this knowledge at his medical follow up for work.

"Willee Mahkray, good to see you. Please, have a seat up on the table."

Willee sat where told and the examiner scanned him with a device he had never seen before. It made his skin heat up, but was without hurt. It beeped, then the assessor looked him in the eye.

"Everything is in order as should be. Perhaps I should explain some of the side effects of Network to you. Many think that tapping in is no different than virtual reality. What actually happens is the switching of places between physical consciousness and spiritual consciousness. The particles that make up the motherboard make the experience supernatural. That's how it opens the mind to creationism. In the physical, you are becoming mechanically dependent. You don't simply connect, The Network becomes you."

"How do you know all this? This is like insider info."

The examiner's features glitched, then arranged to show that the one examining was in fact Zyxira!

"You're him, the one from the television spots."

Zyxira smiled, his olive shade having undertones of orange flashes. His outline was silver. He snapped his fingers and Willee swallowed his tongue. After Mahkray was finished choking, Zyxira dismissed him.

One month after being implanted, Willee found himself void of appetite completely and unable to move his bowels. He found himself missing time. He accepted early retirement shortly after uncovering the meniscal facts behind Networking. He wished he could undo the chip, but he was a segment in the growing hive. He was thankful for house delivery services, as when he would go out places he was followed. He had not only had his voice stolen, but also his ability to write. He was silenced for good. An after effect of the bots in his bloodstream. The secrets of Network was his burden. He helplessly watched as more and more fell for the promised land.

Two months after the insertion of the microchip, Mahkray noticed himself glitching out often. He would walk a few steps then experience full depletion of awareness. Sometimes he would think to walk forward but would go backwards. Other times he was rendered unable to move at all.

He woke up often, seemingly taking frequent naps for unknown periods of length. His dreams were horrific and played out like survival video games. He survived not a single one of the computerized nightmares. His deaths were as endless as those who buried themselves alive in the name of Kommae. Like with his spirit, the only certainty was repose then regeneration.

Four months after getting microchipped, not downlooking would make him deathly ill. The digital withdrawals were unforgiving. He hadn't ate, so he started to vomit out blood and mucus. His veins flowed with micro bots, they were silver with orange flashing. They began to replicate his organs to steel.

By December of that year, Willee was experiencing full out duality. He could no longer function when not hooked up to The Network, not even downlooking kept his sickness at bay. He sat staring and comatose when he wasn't linked in. Even when he felt he was in reality, he still only saw within The Network. His imagination was hacked not by terrorists he once hunted, but by the very one behind everything.

On the last day of the year, Mahkray awoke to the sensation of being weightless. He lifted his arm and saw that his epidermis was slowing disintegrating, there was new skin underneath the stuff withering. A nano layer.

'You are robot,' a voice told him.

He nodded in agreement, totally void of free will.

Chapter 11:

Vengeance Was Mine, Switchery The Second, Mile High Burnings

Zyxira attached the sedated Velocirousel to the glass motherboard. He uploaded it and unleashed a sub series of dimensions. An effect like mirrors within mirrors. The reflections cut through veils and digitalized eras that knew no technologies. It also bore new monsters in varying forms. The Network touched places that Nephaniel never would have thought. It was responsible for transporting the masks that musician ZT had retrieved from overcoming his life lessons, sending them back in time to be worn by a band from Australia. The reflections were ingrained everywhere! The only location not affected was Heaven. All events were infected, and reflecting different outcomes, except for the Crucifixion.

While Zyxira was powered down, Nephaniel's spirit made a visit to Sphere Court. Teleportation was a simple task for a spirit, the thinning veils made it even simpler. He was out for vengeance which also quickened his steps. After drugging Geneva, he walked himself to lot #1. He kicked in the door to find Suzette waiting. She had tubes connected to all her major arteries.

'Looks like a geriatric octopus,' he thought to himself as if he were still one with Zyxira.

"You stubborn prick," she scoffed.

"You knew this day would come," Nephaniel reminded, his face now his own rather than that of Christ.

Some of the tubes took blood away, the others filled her with formaldehyde. She was preserved to death in a second. By time

Nephaniel reached her, she was stiffened and not able to be dismembered.

"NOOOO! VENGEANCE WAS MINE!"

Nephaniel repeated the phrase in sobs and screams until dawn. Nearly being caught when Zyxira rebooted for the day. He missed exploiting himself by a fraction.

Geneva broke the news to Susan, whom had drifted away in her relationship with her mom. Susan then passed the news along to Suzannah who was Suzette's estranged granddaughter.

"No autopsy. She went peacefully, that's all I can say. I'll be forwarding funeral arrangements," was how they were told the news.

Thanks to contests of body counts with the veiled driver, Sphere Court was self sufficient in funds. No lot rent, no taxes. Everything was electric and ran off of the supernatural current.

Suzette would leave her legacy and fortunes to Susan and Suzannah, as well as important roles with the park's cult.

Moxley gave her name to the clinic, but they could not find her appointment. They had to do a hard search of their database to figure out the problem.

"You've already been chipped and were taken out of the appointment."

"You don't understand there's another me. She must have gotten it in my name."

"This is the era of Network, Miss Snygul. There's a second everybody."

"Please, my fridge and cabinets are empty!"

"There's nothing we can do. You already got marked according to us."

Moxley pleaded with the sound of a dial tone for longer than she would want to admit. When she finally heard it, her throat was already hoarse. Her stomach growled so she ate her tears. It was nice to feel some relief against her cracked lips even if the taste was salty.

Exactly when wasn't documented, but once Network took a hold, those who followed Christianity were arrested. It happened fast and quietly. Nobody noticed because everyone was gazing some place else. The majority would have been indifferent to it anyways. Other religions were adaptable, but the Bible warned of what was happening specifically.

"Truth Incineration," Zyxira named the event.

While folks were off exploring and building different sectors of The Network, their bodies were remote controlled by the fingertips of an android. They all attended book burning ceremonies. The only texts burnt were Biblical. If it related to Revelations, it was cast to the fires. The flames rose as tall as the reddening thermometer that sat among the stretching cadavers nailed in their places. Like the temperature reader, the trailers and ones attached were expanding in size. The entirety of Earth quaked for six minutes. Kommae had risen from slumber!

Chapter 12:

Birds Of Flesh, An Unexpected Contact, Order Of The Digital River

Willee Mahkray died in the early hours of his birthday, the year after receiving the mark. His body rotted alone and forgotten, but his spirit rerouted to stay within The Network. He had almost been unable to recall what it was like to be in control of self. It felt good to be back at the wheel, but he was being hunted.

Like all else, the Velocirousel had transformed. The raptors now had replaced their leathery reptilian skin with that of those it had consumed over the years. Red, yellow, black, white, the new look defined terrifying. They were fleshed birds of prey seeking to eat of the spirits. They were still all connected at the spines, not by poles but now chains.

With over half of the population hooked into Network, the need for jobs completely faded. Bills were done away with, as were extracurriculars. Digital funds were driving the marketplace. Businesses had shut down physical locations, everything went online. Like a predictive page from books of Science Fiction, cars could fly, humanity was diminishing, the lines between what thought real and what was called make believe were blurred and robots were possessing Earth! The future seen by writers was now at hand thanks to the other realm. The Network drove the lives of millions. Despite it being full of entities, wherever Willee was there wasn't any others. He had been driven to no man's land.

Reversed carnival music played as he walked along trees made up of glass shards. If he would have touched a single twig, he would have been brought to another parallel to where he was. They looked sharp, so he avoided their touch, foregoing escape. The bark shards were crafted from the shattered mirrors of the Velocirousel. Being so, the raptors could travel via their interiors. The trunks burst without warning, loosening the epidermis covered dinosaurs. Willee ran, but the jaws of the dinos were unending. They snapped at his heels, only missing because of their spinal chains that pulled them backwards, as the others attempted their own bites. One snap after another. When he reached a dead end among the path of trees, he knew he would be devoured. The snarling predator slashed its claw against one of the trees causing two shards to fly and stick into Willee's eyeballs. The shards then reflected his first day in The Network before his line of sight.

He was sitting on the back porch of a castle with pretty ladies all around his arena sized pool. They were flirty and were teasing so he suggested they all jump in the water to do so. When the females did as told, he filled the pool with microscopic sharks that nibbled the women to particles. Some of the ladies attempted to get out of the infested waters but the mini sharks were able to bite their way up their bodies and ended their pursuits of fleeing. When they were all dead, he imagined a moptopus to clean up the gory mess. As the mopping was taking place, Mahkray watched the traffic jam in the sky.

Once the blood and particles were mopped up, he returned before the ravaging reptile. He was then half gobbled by the raptor clothed in the flesh of Kipley. It was bigger than the others and the dominant one. Willee's other half was consumed once his scraps were left alone. The rest of the pack wasted no time in ensuring nothing remained.

What Moxley seen as unfair was actually a blessing under the surface. The Network only existed in Earth two. The fact that the doppelganger was from the third Earth had caused another disruption of reflections. In doing this, she had undone a video she had hid away. Yelxom had tried to screw her other half over by taking her mark, but had actually helped the other her figure out some of what puzzled her. By end of the transmission, Moxley was relieved she had not taken the chip.

The transmission was one from a kid known as Truk Nosmada of Earth three. He had managed to escape from his holding cell as he was awaiting his death sentence. He then recorded an accidental glimpse of what he saw behind the scenes of the microchips and Network. He tried to send it, but it was intercepted by Yelxom. She then turned the young lad back in. Truk was an interdimensional vagabond who had dedicated his life to exploiting what was behind the veils. He drifted to all types of realms and was a nuisance to those who wanted to quiet talks of other existences. His sentencing was moved forward once he was caught and it was carried out a few years later when he was an infant. In Earth three, they age inverted of second Earth.

Truk was six at the moment of the recording.

The transcript of the transmission:

"I hope this message reaches Moxley Snygul. If it does not, please locate her and show her this imperative video. Hi, Moxley. So much to explain, but the clock is ticking. This is Truk Nosmada, I reside in Earth three. I look like a child, but believe that I have lived out most of my life. Years ago, I invented a special pair of contacts that acted as cameras. I saw things that completely destroyed my thinking of reality and what lies past it. During these travels, I also stumbled on the truth behind the future marking of people on your Earth. To accept the microchip is to sell the soul. It will rid you of your humanity and turn you to a mindless bot. The one you worship is not messianic, he is a droid. His desire is to eradicate humans. He is stealing the imagery of God and sealing his own creation on Earth. Listen close, those with dents in their pinkies were guineas and all lost their lives to The Ne..."

The transmission was cut short when a brigade of robots busted his door down and seized him. Truk was able to press the send button as they hauled him off.

Moxley stewed over the communication meant for her. She remembered noticing a matching indentation on her step mother's pinky shortly before finding out her adopted parent was dead. She thought about the TV appearances from Zyxira, then how the communication stated he was evil and wanted genocide. She stopped and truly looked around at what was going on and wanted nothing to do with it. She repented for ever thinking to give place to it all. She was raised in church, but left after she was strapped to a retired electric chair as a teen. She retained tiny bits from the sermon during her seating, mainly "Repentance" and "Hell." Her stint in the chair wasn't long, but everything about those moments stuck.

Nephaniel's spirit longed for control again. It was getting cramped inside of the silver lined mechanical messiah. One of the reflections that happened after uploading the Velocirousel, was Nephaniel from third Earth was killed and his spirit was given unto Nephaniel of Earth two. Zyxira didn't notice the shift since the energy remained unchanged. The vibrations matched. Zyxira was none the wiser.

Zyxira kept himself out of Network, they both knew the wonders there were on autopilot towards the climax, so Nephaniel's spirit knew he was safe inside of it if he managed to not get entrapped. He could easily tap in being not of dermis, it was a spirit world after all. He molded himself into a clone of Jesus and gave an emergency speech to those online.

"Offspring of The Network, take heed to this message. There is a battalion coming here. They're going to unplug us all permanently. Avoidance can only be attained by means of suicide. There's a digital river flowing in the data stream, go to it and drown yourselves. Commit to Network and you shall never depart from it!"

The majority listened and the cyber inlet filled with floating spirits. Those who were faithful's physical forms turned to walking computers with total reliance on currents to sustain life. They were robots.

With the retinas of the drowned, Nephaniel was able to print himself a body outside of The Network. This was his calling that the robotic impostor was living. Unlike with Suzette, he would avenge what was rightfully his. It was his ring the world would kiss, the rusted scroll had promised so. He had to be the one to deliver the cooked planet to The Pit, not another.

Those pinned looked at Nephaniel and whispered, "you should not be here," with their crusty, blackened mouths. He brushed past their elongated limbs as they grasped for him. Being melted on, their reach wasn't far anyhow. They disbelieved that it could be him and desired to confirm by feeling his scars. They saw him as resurrected.

"Deliver us," their shriveled lips demanded.

He tread on bloody soles, determined to locate Zyxira. He used the other inner him as a tracking device. He could tell the intersections were starting to blend, the danger levels were higher than he had ever seen them before. Since he was again covered with flesh, his prime meat attracted all the things that lurked among the dimensions. The weakened barriers were a positive omen to him. The hour was drawing late for Earth and shortening!

Chapter 13:

Collecting On A Previous Agreement, What Is Required Now Is Large-scale Surgery

Zyxira passed a popular vlogger as he made his way to G.M.S. headquarters.

"Good day, sir," Cog Nictiv greeted, not knowing who he was passing.

Zyxira ignored the petty human. He heard a scuffle, then turned and laughed. The exclaim was forced but reflected how he thought he felt. Lasers had blasted Cog apart. Bloody debris littered the sidewalk.

"Not for you, meat slabs," the android joked without a laugh.

He walked to the entrance and let himself in. He knew where he was headed. He stormed his way there and was met by the boss of the company.

"Well, if it isn't the man who granted me fortune and fame. Come to put what you had me build to use?"

"Rhetorical question presumed."

G.M. pricked his finger and let a drop of blood authenticate entry.

The two went in and stood before the circular gateway. The outer frame of the gate was revolving and clicking like a safe trying to crack itself. After six revolutions, it started to open. Zyxira squirmed with anticipation.

"Looks like a birth canal," Zyxira exclaimed happily.

"That's literally what you stated to me I was architecting here," G.M. smirked.

"Shhhhh. I can hear The Pause coming! There's lot of doors and windows, but this one conquers them all."

G.M. felt a bit nervous about what this madman was up to. He could hear something coming up the tunnel as well. The sounds emitting definitely were not human! Zyxira was fully welcoming the coming.

"Arise! Arise!"

G.M. walked next to the opening and leaned in.

"I wouldn't get too close," Zyxira warned.

"What's that sound? Is it munching on something?"

Zyxira's eyes lit up orange and glowed. The whole area was lit by his excitement. Then, the head of a serpent poked through. Like The Totter of Sphere Court, its spine was on the outside of its body and was curved. Coiled might be a better term. Either way, the spine was basically like a giant slinky.

"Are you aware there have been three incarnations of Earth?"

"Can't say I did, bud."

"In the first one, blood usually ran red but sometimes, when the air quality was too high or low, they would bleed silver."

"Ok then."

"Just a random that popped in," Zyxira shrugged, turning his gaze back to Kommae.

When the buried one was fully out, it took up the wholeness of the large room. Even coiled several times, The Pause was massive. At the other end of the spine was a pair of pinchers. Similar to that of an insect but literally two huge fingers! It walked on human arms and hands, thousands of them. Zyxira had laid a trail of bait for the Kommae to enjoy as a welcome gift. The path had consisted of carrions. It was their limbs that lifted The Pause so that he need not slither.

While anti-discrimination laws were being passed for the Miscreated race, the Networkers desired a physical mutation of their own. Zyxira was tickled to learn of this. He consulted his pal Gynor, who had some insane ideas himself. They used the GPS to locate each member that showed interest and they all willingly underwent surgery.

Upon awakening, the new forms found themselves unable to speak aloud. Their tongues had been replaced with ten inch extension cords. The removed detail was a small matter to them who had been typing and texting for most of their lives. They could now perform the tasks without having to clack away at keys. Speech was not the only thing different. They also had to charge for twelve hours to function. Lack of a full charge meant zilch for energy. Aside from this, they also no longer saw in color. Yet another side effect that didn't matter. Forms of discrimination went away, both in and out of Network. Zyxira was programming it so. His march was not for equality though, he did this for the sake of dominion. He was being served as God had once been. Adored for his ability to bring unity. These were creations in his image. His reflection of the power of God.

As was done with Drayton years before, the Networkers responded with nothing more than a flick of a fingertip. Not just within their physical forms, but also the other realm now. Mind and body controlled completely. He brought to life each one's fears, diving deep to manifest what he made be that tormented the Networkers. He blocked their ability to unplug so he could enjoy using people as marionettes and their despair would enable the absorbing Kommae. Slavery was back full swing and everyone was too enveloped in The Network to see things as they were. Even if they unplugged, most would deny what they saw. All these things were just mirrored photons, nothing unseen. Mere surfaces of the former bouncing back at different angles.

Chapter 14:
Crematory Appliances

Network Society demanded that Zyxira do something to convert those marked to be more like the walking computers who had drowned themselves at Nephaniel's bidding. The surgeries were a step forward, but it was not enough. He was bombarded with emails. Another push for the extinction of God's blueprint. Zyxira felt no pressure, he had been planning this very thing for years. Among those making protest was a blind community of Klyne County. The only member to not fuss about it was named Jeremy. He had a copy of a Bible in braille prior to the mile high burnings. He was burned alive along with his treasured book after he refused to release it from his grip. They were cast into the flames and many rejoiced because of it.

The blind community wasn't passed over, Gynor was saving the best for last.

"Anything he from Bethlehem can do, we can do better," Zyxira remarked.

The android and Gynor, the latter who was undergoing his formation as an insect, broadcasted to the world. All stations carried the broadcast, all Networkers were tuned in without option.

"My people, I have wonderful news regarding evolutionary measures. Many of you reached out to me about further transformation. All cities may have noticed structures appearing. If you haven't, you will. Gynor has developed Crematory Appliances. Most of you are unaware, but the bottom layer of your skin has been built as nano. You will all go to the Appliances to take the next step."

Zyxira had expected his tongue to translate to the specific languages of wherever it was being watched. His inbox blowing up a second time let him know that his ability had not been working. He tried to reach the spirit inside without luck. Gynor used his dissimulation invention to try to unconnect the two but couldn't. The droid felt nothing, although he sought fury. He commanded those able to translate the good news to do so, which they did promptly.

The Crematories looked like sizable toasters. They acted in the same way. Networkers were lined up as bread, lowered and heated for purpose of flesh removal. The heat cooled in their cranium and formed the galvanized fluid in to microchips.

"Felt like I was born again," many of the Networkers described.

Zyxira had prepared a path of body parts to lead Kommae to the trailer park with the sidewall sacrifices. He had not been back in awhile. When he revisited, he found three significant things.

The first one, was another shift of the mobile homes. They had rearranged to create the shape of a 'S.' Kommae had crawled through the centers of the wheeled houses and was absorbing the energies from the spirits. Though they felt uplifted, but their energy was actually despair. They weren't created for this and the blasphemy helped The Pause to start to grow. They grew in unity, stretching with fierce growing pains.

The second and third thing, caused Zyxira's electrodes to fume. Standing next to a yellow thermometer was Nephaniel! He was staring at his android counterpart, holding one of the elastic hands of Dawna.

"Bold to defy," Zyxira growled in the voice he was built with.

"This was to be mine. All of it."

"Never was yours."

"Geneva is closer to winning. Look at the color, you've failed!"

"Let her have her moment. It's nothing. Whom we serve is supreme!"

"He is glorious, huh?"

Nephaniel's tone softened as he looked at the swaying pins that were serving their function. He let go of his sister, then put his palm against

The Pause. The scales were not slippery or dry, they were metallic. They moved when he touched them as if liquid steel. The spines looked as barium. His body was consolidating the trailers against the coiled vertebrae, using the metal, and those attached, as armor.

Zyxira sighed. Like it or not, Nephaniel and him were in conjunction. Their goal was their common. What mattered now was that they see their objective to cessation.

"Where do we go from here, brother?"

"Consummation."

Chapter 15:
Conflict Of Four, M.A.S.S. Decreed

There had been gossip overseas around the region where Jesus once walked. Two men were trying to persuade Networkers to renounce their faith. After three years of hearing about the two commanding rainfall, striking cities with plagues and eliminating their enemies with breath of white fire, Zyxira and Nephaniel went to see for themselves about the fuss.

The two men were fearless in their prophesying. They walked the streets preaching and stirred up quite the commotion when their witnessing was ignored. Anyone who harmed them was crisped out of their way. For six months Nephaniel and the android followed the two from afar. While they admired the men's courage, they were also weary in their patience levels. The duet needed dealt with.

In the sixth month, fifteen days in, on a Wednesday, Zyxira went before a well that was said to spew blood. He called down in the well and was answered by an one eyed Geneva Shaw. Her image was reflected to where he was via the well.

"You've seen better days," the droid innuendoed.

"Eye no time for your foolery," Geneva punned.

Their expressions stayed dry as they played on words. Neither found joy in the verbiage.

"Forgive my intrusion, but I have something to request of you."

"Quickly. You still owe me as it is."

"I need you to summon the one from the bottomless."

Geneva grinned a vile smirk. Her eye rolled back and she began to speak in demonic tongues. Chains could be heard falling off of something inside the well as she gave up villainous syllables. The two witnesses also heard the loosening of the binds and made their way to the bleeding well.

"In the name of Jesus Christ, we demand you to cease," they demanded simultaneously.

Two clawed hands grabbed on either side of the well, then a black beast rose up, splashing silver blood all around the entrance to the bottomless. It roared at the two men of light, but they stood their ground. Neither of them rebuked it, which was a mystery to Zyxira and Nephaniel.

The beast leapt towards the witnesses for Godliness. Zyxira went live with his eyes, broadcasting the circumstance to his followers. The beast had six eyes that were attached to thin pieces of metal that orbited its head. It had no features, only a frame of darkness. Without budge, the two men were slaughtered. The beast tore each limb off, then their heads. The voice of a woman beckoned the beast back into the bottomless, but it wasn't that of Geneva. It was the vocals of The Deep.

For three and a half days, the men laid strewn across the ground in gory detail. The Networkers rejoiced and partied at the resistance's grisly residue, even exchanging presents in celebration. Zyxira continued to stream the bloody mess, while Nephaniel rolled himself in their DNA. He drank and ate of them also. All done in mockery.

Twelve hours in to the fourth day, a bright fire swarmed around the scattered parts of the witnesses and made them whole again. They stood before Zyxira and Nephaniel with their heads held high. The Networkers were frightened by the resurrection. A loud voice boomed from Heaven and took the resurrected men away in a cloud. The city where they laid dead quaked viciously once they were gone, seven thousand were killed as a result. Among the deceased was Nephaniel. His skull was crushed by many rocks. Lots of people who lived in the city denied The Network and repented before God, which infuriated Zyxira. He took it upon himself to implement a new worldwide law.

"God thinks that he has the upper hand, my children. What are we to do but provide his arrogance at fault? Every Saturday from here to Armageddon, you all will participate in upgrades to your skeletons. Let heaven see that you defy his image. We are not holy. We are heathen. In the name of Network, you are immortalized. Shed your natural forms and become made in my image!"

The earthquake had removed half of Zyxira's Christ covering. He now more resembled Jesus as He hung on the cross. With his clay suit in shambles, his people could now see the blue, silver lined, robot underneath. Periodically, they would see orange flashes.

Lucifer came to assist Zyxira by possessing the spirit of Nephaniel from third Earth. Together they spent a week reassembling the antenna that Nephaniel had built. The earthquake had taken down the structure. When it was repaired without flaw, Lucifer ripped the spirit from Zyxira. The droid thanked his fallen angelic partner and shook his slimy hand. There was no ridiculous pitchfork or spaded tail. Lucifer was the father of lies. He looked hairy from afar, but he wasn't made up of hair. The strands were all tongues. Millions of pink tongues clothed the defiled musician. He took the spirit of the other Nephaniel to the outer darkness of space and left him to drown eternally. An anchor was wrapped around the spirit's throat.

On Saturday, Zyxira stood among the now towering Kommae. The nailed corpses looked dried up and stretched out, but still lifted their songs with praise. The android flipped the switch and a grand noise of static came over the entire Earth, not only the second but also the third. The only place the noise wasn't heard was Sphere Court. The antenna shot the wet electricity into the sky which responded with silver thunder. The thunder clapped in a frightening manner. The physical bodies of the Networkers all began to walk towards the source of the static. Then, the silver was overtaken by red and lightning began to strike into the microchip brains, attaching and changing their bones to titanium. Coding their thoughts.

Zyxira stood emotionless and stared up at the sky in defiance. He hoped God was watching and weeping.

Chapter 16:

Fallout From Sphere Court

Zyxira may have been winning the battle, but the same could not be said for Htaed or Geneva Shaw. The face of The Deep was broken, God still was the authority. White flames, much resembling the ones that resurrected the witnesses, shot down into the well within Sphere Court. The fire shot into the clouds causing white thunder. Bright lightening then came from the sky and attached to the mechanical minds of the Networkers. The attachments turned the mechanics back to mortal. For a temporary time, the Networkers saw Earth as God had in the beginning. They saw through the retinas of light. When the light stopped, silence fell over the lands and waters of the third planet. Not third in the sense as most astronomers claim, but third in the sense of planets that underwent decimation. The thermometer slowly began to darken. Sand grains were few in number for Earth.

Chapter 17:

Totalitarianism Shall Be Law, 144K Edges And Buckets

The game of Earthly jurisdiction continued to press on. Zyxira knew his time length was thinning, Lucifer knew it too. They wrote it as law that mankind had to be marked. To not league with The Network meant certain demise. Most had never left the other realm anyways and their physical eyes reflected the fact. Some had rejoined, only to convert themselves to Christianity after a computer virus exposed them to the truth behind everything. One hundred and forty four thousand were their number. Drones filled the sky and hunted down those who opposed. Trapping them in confinement lasers, the prisoners were put in isolation camps to await their beheadings. Among the imprisoned was the one who had built the very drones that arrested him, G.M. of G.M.S. Incorporated. Nobody was above the new law.

The majority reluctantly reconnected to The Network. They feared not existing more than an eternity of Hellfire. An abyss of insectoid drones were released. They were hideous to behold. Their bodies full of bugged eyes, their dangling stingers were syringes. They flew to each obedient Networker and stung them. Those jabbed cried out in anguish. The Networkers were remarked with fresh glass barcodes once the pain dimmed. The new marks were monitored by Zyxira directly, wirelessly connect to his motherboard. They mimicked his movements, mirroring his every move. He marched into the oceans and they all did the same. He was holding on to his deal struck with Geneva. This was her fail safe. The second empowering of The Deep to eliminate the light.

Guillotines appeared all over the second Earth. Then, the decapitations of the saints began. Like with the two witnesses, the murders were streamed live to the Networkers. Two extra people were added to the number beheaded, the duo who were behind the virus that was released. All of the dismemberments were stored in their own respective buckets.

The moon turned to blood, reddening with the Bloodline of God that was denied elsewhere. Though thousands reverted back to human, millions still aligned with The Network and Zyxira.

The sky then turned red itself, as the second M.A.S.S. began. The crimson lightning began to attack the sun, resulting in a supernova. The star exploded and a dragon flew out from it. It was composed of the bloody shards of the headless martyrs, another reflection. Lucifer rode on its back and the dragon ate what was in the one hundred and forty four thousand buckets.

Chapter 18:
Armageddon, Wormwood, Back To Orange

During the second M.A.S.S., a vacuum salesman caused a grand hum to fill the ears of all on Earth, both the second and third. For the first time, both Earths experienced the exact same thing. Armageddon was given sovereignty. Simultaneous with the revelation of the salesman's latest invention came World War III. A nuke labelled, 'Wormwood,' was detonated which crashed The Network and poisoned a majority of Earth two's waters. *The Event* was reflected into the third Earth when an interdimensional spider poisoned the woman who had eaten its inhabitants. As she lay dying, so did the Networkers.

"Everything reflects," Zyxira reminded his programming as white zolts from Heaven stripped him of what was left of his disguise.

Zyxira burst with electricity which fried his cult that were lining the ocean floor. Those who had not marched into the depths were all torn to bits by the nuclear blast. Glitches of raptors came and went, feeding, disposing of the evidence of mankind and The Network. Earth sat in the cosmic waters, void and without form. All water evaporated that was on Earth and began to heat with the fires of Hell.

Swimming in the watery cosmos, using the devoured's limbs like paddles, was The Pause. Kommae was now twice as big as planet Earth and sitting in wait. His armor was a combination of burnt sacrifice and twisted metal, the barium spine still protruded through on the outside of his frame. The dead's lips moved but the waters stole their sound. The thermometer turned a gloomy orange and started to darken. Kommae's mouth opened, then he waited for the shade to go red so he could feast one final time.

Moxley's rebellion went unknown, the other her had replaced her and in doing so set her free of the tribulations of the mark. She watched as the Earth flashed over and over as computers and breakers burst. The dark age had begun. She stood in the blackness and sobbed. Terrible scuffles arose from all around her, the dimensions were no more. She was pulled at from all sides, then a bright fire engulfed her without burning her. Her skin was removed, then she was not. Taken like a thief in the night.

The glass demons went to the outer layer of the firmament and surrounded the globe. They turned themselves to satellites and called out to the light. They wanted the last pound of flesh.

"Only spirits may dwell in heaven," they beamed.

"The one whom did not meet death must be sent back!"

The Almighty sighed and looked at the girl running to the outland of Heaven. He was ready for Judgment Day, but the nagging shards were correct. There was still one with a body of clay. He waved His hand and it was so. An interdimensional scale appeared, half in Heaven, half on Earth. The altar of Hemmoraging. The running girl would close the chapter of flesh. God lingered in wait, so did the dark ones who were now roaming free.

Don't miss out!

Visit the website below and you can sign up to receive emails whenever Christopher Besonen publishes a new book. There's no charge and no obligation.

https://books2read.com/r/B-A-NQAP-WIBUB

BOOKS 2 READ

Connecting independent readers to independent writers.

www.ingramcontent.com/pod-product-compliance
Lightning Source LLC
Chambersburg PA
CBHW020748160726
47993CB00006B/2668